FEARFUL MEETS DISMISSIVE
When Insecurity Faces Independence

The Attachment Drama Healing Series ™

Therapeutic Relationship Fiction ™

JOHANNA SPARROW

FEARFUL MEETS DISMISSIVE When Insecurity Faces Independence The Attachment Drama Healing Series ™ Therapeutic Relationship Fiction ™ **Copyright © 2026 by Antoinette Maria Watkins**

All rights reserved. No part of this publication may be reproduced, distributed, or transmitted in any form or by any means, including photocopying, recording, or other electronic or mechanical methods, without the prior written permission of the publisher, except in the case of brief quotations used in reviews, critical articles, or educational settings as permitted by copyright law.

This book is a work of fiction blended with therapeutic concepts. Names, characters, places, events, and incidents are products of the author's imagination or are used fictitiously. Any resemblance to actual persons, living or dead, or actual events is purely coincidental.

Published by Blue Shoes Publishing
www.BlueShoesPublishing.com

Cover and Interior Design: Blue Shoes Publishing
Author: Johanna Sparrow (Pen Name)
Legal Copyright Holder: Antoinette Maria Watkins

ISBN (Paperback): 978-1-967148-59-2
ISBN (eBook): 978-1-967148-61-5

Printed in the United States of America

First Edition: 2026

DEDICATION

For everyone learning to love through their fears—
may this journey remind you that healing is possible,
even when your heart is unsure.

Author's Note

Fearful Meets Dismissive is the first released story in **The Attachment Drama Healing Series™**, my world of **Therapeutic Relationship Fiction™**—where fiction and emotional healing meet on purpose. I didn't write this book just for fun or entertainment, even though I absolutely want you to enjoy Craig and Demi's journey. I wrote it as a mirror, a soft landing place, and a guided invitation to look at your own patterns in love without shame or guilt.

This series was born from years of listening to people say things like, "Why do I always fall for the same type?" "Why do I run when things get real?" or "Why do I crave closeness and then feel like I can't handle it?"

In Craig and Demi, I chose to start with a potent mix: **fearful-avoidant** and **dismissive-avoidant** energy colliding in one relationship. Their story is emotional, raw, and messy at times—but so is healing. As you read, you'll notice the story isn't just told; it's **processed** through reflection sections, self-inquiry prompts, and gentle emotional coaching woven into the narrative. That's the heart of what **Therapeutic Relationship Fiction™** is all about.

This is the **first release story** in the Attachment Drama Healing Series™, but it is **not** the beginning and end of the healing framework. A deeper, more structured guide is on its way to help you understand your attachment styles.

Very soon, you'll see the **foundation** book that sits underneath all of these stories—the one that names the patterns, explains the attachment dynamics, and walks you step-by-step through the **Attachment Drama Healing Method** I use throughout this universe. Where *Fearful Meets Dismissive* lets you feel the journey through characters. The foundation book will help you:

- Understand why you and the people you love behave the way you do in relationships
- Identify your attachment patterns and the "emotional contracts" you keep repeating
- Begin practicing simple, real-world tools to create safer, more secure connections

If you resonated with Demi's craving for closeness or Craig's pull toward distance, you are already doing the work—you're recognizing yourself. That's where healing starts.

Thank you for starting this journey with me here, at the intersection of story and self-work. This series will grow into something bigger than one book: more couples, more patterns, more mirrors, and more tools to help you unlearn what fear taught you about love.

My hope is simple:

As you move through these pages, you don't just read about Craig and Demi healing—you begin to **heal with them.**

With gratitude,
Johanna Sparrow

Coming Soon: Foundation Book

Coming Soon in The Attachment Drama Healing Series™

The Attachment Drama Healing Method
Foundation Book – Coming Early 2026

Step behind the scenes of *Fearful Meets Dismissive* and into the core framework that shapes every story in **The Attachment Drama Healing Series™**.

In **The Attachment Drama Healing Method**, you'll:
- Learn the key attachment styles and how fearful, dismissive, anxious, and secure energies show up in real-life relationships.
- Discover practical tools to soothe your nervous system, break old patterns, and build safer, more secure connections.
- Explore reflection prompts, exercises, and healing pathways that complement the emotional journeys you experience in the fiction books.

If Fearful Meets Dismissive helped you see your patterns, the foundation book will help you **understand and transform them**.
Look for **The Attachment Drama Healing Method in early 2026**—

....continue your journey from avoidant love to healing love.

Table of Contents

Introduction
1. The Distance Between Us
2. Fragile Ground
3. Unspoken Rules
4. The Walls We Build
5. Trigger Points
6. The Space Between
7. Crossroads
8. The Mirror Work
9. The Reconnection
10. Love in Real Time
11. Triggers and Truths
12. Safe Space
13. Old Wounds, New Patterns
14. Relearning Intimacy
15. The Setback
16. The Repair Ritual
17. The Vulnerability Pact
18. The Secure Space
19. Integration
20. Full Circle

Epilogue
Acknowledgments
About the Author
Resources & Further Reading

Introduction
When Avoidance Meets Love

Some love stories start with a spark; others begin with silence. This one starts somewhere in between, you know, in that uncertain space where two hearts want to connect but don't know how.

You've probably felt it yourself — that push and pull between wanting closeness and fearing it. Maybe you've been the one reaching out, only to watch someone you love withdraw. Or perhaps you're the one who needs to step back when things get too intense, even though you crave connection and acceptance.

Craig and Demi's story is not about heroes and villains. It's about patterns — fearful and dismissive patterns — that keep love at arm's length. Craig, with his careful control and emotional walls, represents the dismissive-avoidant personality type. Demi, passionate yet anxious, embodies the fearful-avoidant, torn between wanting love and fearing rejection.

Together, they'll teach us how avoidance can masquerade as protection — and how healing begins when we dare to unlearn what once kept us safe through unhealthy patterns.

As you move through each chapter, you'll find yourself in their story — maybe in their silence, trauma, their missteps, or their breakthroughs. And after each part, you'll find a **Reflection Section** to help you turn their lessons into your own healing practice so that you can win at love.

You're not reading about them. You're healing with them.

Are you ready to start healing?

Chapter One

The Distance Between Us

The café was half-empty, the kind of place where the humming of the espresso machine fills the silence you're too afraid to break or even say a word. That's where Craig first noticed a woman with tired eyes that still somehow glowed with curiosity. Demi was the woman he didn't approach that day.

    Dismissive attachment styles rarely do. Instead, Craig tucked her image away, quietly admiring the way she seemed both open and guarded while looking around the café. There was something familiar in that — something he couldn't name.
    Weeks later, fate (or maybe habit) placed them in the same line at the corner bookstore. She dropped a book. He picked it up. Their conversation was easy at first, but underneath it, both hearts raced for different reasons.
    Craig feared needing anyone. Demi feared being too much and that love avoided her.
    They exchanged numbers but hesitated to use them. The silence between texts stretched out longer than either admitted.
And yet, neither could let the other go.

Something about their distance felt... safe and fearful at the same time.
It was as if they'd both found a version of love that didn't demand too much closeness, nor acceptance, something Demi craved.
And t

hat, right there, was the problem, especially for Demi, who wanted acceptance.

Reflection Section — Why We Keep Our Distance

Avoidance is not a lack of love; it's a fear of being seen.
For fearful and dismissive avoidants, love is both the medicine and the trigger.

Fearful-avoidant reflection: You crave closeness, but when someone gets too close, it feels unsafe, so you push them away. Your mind says, "I want love," but your body says, "Run."
Healing focus: Learn to soothe the fear underneath your craving. Closeness is not danger; it's discomfort healing in real time.
Dismissive-avoidant reflection: You value independence so deeply that needing someone feels like weakness. But disconnection isn't control; it is loneliness dressed up as strength, yet you tell yourself it's normal to feel this way.
Healing focus: Let yourself rely on others in small, safe ways. Needing someone does not diminish your power — it deepens and strengthens your connection with others.

Exercise:
Write about a time when you kept emotional distance, even from someone who made you feel safe. What were you protecting yourself from? Why were you afraid?

Chapter Two
Fragile Ground

The first time Craig let Demi into his apartment, he noticed how her eyes moved — scanning the space like it was a test she wasn't sure she'd pass, and she had every right to fear Craig, since he was no different from other men she liked and had hurt her. Everything about her energy suggested caution; even though she was trying to appear comfortable, she was not.

She commented on his minimalist décor — neutral colors, sparse furniture, everything in its place. It wasn't just neat; it was defensive. There were no signs of vulnerability — no photos, no clutter, no softness.

"Feels... peaceful," she said, though what she meant was lonely.
He smiled politely. "I like quiet," he replied.

Demi nodded, even though being quiet made her anxious and uncomfortable. Silence left too much room for thought — for rejection to echo in her head.

They talked over coffee. Craig asked her about work; she shared stories that skimmed the surface. Whenever she got too close to revealing emotion, he'd change the subject, and she'd let him.

It was like watching two dancers afraid to step on each other's toes — graceful, cautious, and exhausting all at the same time.

Later, when she left, Craig stood by the window, staring at the city lights. He felt relief that the evening went "smoothly," but under that calm surface was a pang of emptiness.

He didn't want to need her.

But he didn't want her to go, either.

And Demi? She walked home feeling the same contradiction. She wanted to feel chosen, but she feared pushing too hard. She texted him, *"Thanks for tonight,"* then stared at the screen, waiting for a reply that didn't come until morning.

That's what fragile ground feels like — two people balancing between fear and desire, both hoping the other one will be brave first.

Reflection Section — When Connection Feels Unsafe

Avoidant relationships often begin like this: both people trying to connect while protecting their wounds.
The dance is subtle — one partner fears closeness, the other fears abandonment. Both are reacting, not relating.

Fearful-Avoidant Insight:
You may find yourself overanalyzing every silence, every delay in response, because your body remembers inconsistency. You might fear that love always comes with rejection and that rejection hurts like hell.

Healing focus: Slow down your interpretations. Silence isn't always abandonment. Sometimes it's someone's fear speaking, not their lack of care.

Dismissive-Avoidant Insight:
You might feel suffocated when someone wants more connection. You don't mean to withdraw, but emotional intensity triggers your need for control. It's about staying safe and balanced.

Healing focus: Before pulling away, ask yourself, "*Am I protecting my peace or avoiding vulnerability?*" The two often feel the same, but they lead to very different outcomes.

Reflection Exercise:
Write down what "safety" in a relationship means to you. Then ask: Does your definition of safety leave room for intimacy, or does it keep people out?

Chapter Three
Unspoken Rules

There was a rhythm to Craig and Demi's interactions — a quiet agreement neither had spoken aloud, not yet at least.

They didn't call too often. They didn't ask too many questions. They didn't press for more; caution was in the air, and it felt safe.

Every conversation had a ceiling.

Every text had a pause.

They were both following a set of **unspoken rules** designed to protect them from the thing they secretly wanted most — closeness, love, and acceptance.

It started one evening when Demi texted, *"You've been quiet. Nothing to say, and is everything okay?"*

Craig stared at his phone, thumb hovering over the keyboard. His instinct was to say *I'm fine* — the classic dismissive cover that works so well in the past— but he wasn't. Work had been heavy, his sleep was shallow, and he didn't know how to let someone into that space.

He typed, *"Just busy. You?"*

Demi read his reply twice. It was polite, distant. She told herself not to take it personally, but she sensed that something was amiss. *He's probably tired. Please don't make it about you, but she did, like always.*

But deep down, it already was about her — or rather, about the part of her that always felt like she was asking for too much, if not too needy.

She didn't text back right away. She waited. Hours passed. And that silence — it was loud enough to make Craig feel both guilt and relief.

He wanted her to care, but not too much.

He wanted space, but not emptiness.

Unspoken rules kept them safe — or so they thought.

No "good morning" texts unless the other started first.

No vulnerability unless the mood felt light.

No bringing up feelings if it might change the vibe, and Craig had no part in emotions.

They were building a connection out of caution instead of courage.

Days later, they met for dinner. Conversation was easy — safe topics, laughter where it belonged. But when Demi mentioned something real — how her ex made her feel invisible — Craig felt a twinge of discomfort. He changed the subject to something neutral, like a show on Netflix, his go-to escape from dealing with what was right in front of him— a connection.

And she let him. She smiled and followed his lead as she had done time and time again.

Neither of them realized that silence, too, can be a rule — one they'd been obeying all their lives.

Reflection Section — The Cost of Emotional Safety

Unspoken rules are a defense mechanism. They exist because, at some point, open expression no longer felt safe.

When two avoidant partners meet, they often create a contract of distance — quiet, respectful, and emotionally underfed.

Fearful-Avoidant Insight:
You crave connection but anticipate rejection. That makes you shrink before you can be hurt. You may "mirror" your partner's withdrawal to avoid looking needy. You fear love, but it's all you think about.

Healing focus: Notice when silence is fear, not peace. When you want to reach out but don't, ask yourself — What story am I telling myself about what might happen if I do?

Dismissive-Avoidant Insight:
You maintain space because it feels like control. But this control often keeps you disconnected from emotional nourishment.

Healing focus: Practice tolerating closeness in small doses. Respond a little sooner, share a little more, let one truth out — even if it feels uncomfortable. This can help you connect your emotions to what is real.

Johanna's Reflection:
Love doesn't grow in spaces where both people are too careful. You can't build intimacy and safety if honesty feels like danger.

Start small. Speak one truth that breaks an unspoken rule — not to challenge love, but to deepen it. Your truth should be honesty.

🗒 Self-Reflection Prompt:
What "rules" do you silently follow in relationships?
Who taught you that being easy to love meant being easy to handle?

Chapter Four
The Walls We Build

Craig stayed far away from any form of therapy because it pulled at his emotions. What he believed in kept him busy, such as working hard and keeping his feelings to himself, like neatly folded laundry on a shelf, because he was in control and it kept him safe. He did not have time for heartfelt situations, wrapped in emotion, yet his old tricks no longer worked with Demi.

He began to realize that something was wrong, even if he was not yet ready for change.

The nights were too quiet. The walls of Craig's apartment — once a comfort — now felt like a reminder of everything Craig kept out.

When Demi came over one Friday evening, she noticed the tension before he spoke. "Rough week?" she asked gently, without being too noisy.

He hesitated. "Just work," he said, but his voice lacked conviction.

She sat beside him on the couch. "You don't have to talk about it," she offered, meaning the opposite and hoping he would open up to her.

"I'm fine," he repeated — and even he didn't believe it this time, but he had to maintain control of his emotions.

Silence stretched between them. Demi felt her chest tighten — that familiar panic that told her she was losing him. She started filling the space with questions, trying to find a way in.

But every question hit a wall; he was not letting her into his space, not now and not ever.

Craig felt cornered, even though she wasn't attacking. He stood up, walked to the kitchen, muttering something about needing water.

Demi sat back, exhaling quietly. She wasn't angry. She was tired — tired of tiptoeing around invisible boundaries. Tired of pretending the distance didn't hurt, unsure if she should get up and walk out.

When he returned, she said softly, "You don't always have to be okay, you know."

He looked at her then — really looked — but his defenses were louder than her compassion.

"I don't do feelings like that," he said.

And Demi smiled the kind of smile people use to hide heartbreak.

"I know," she whispered.

That night, when she left, Craig watched her go, the walls of his apartment closing in tighter than ever. For the first time, he wondered if emotional safety had become his prison and if Demi would return.

Reflection Section — The Function of Walls

Walls are built for protection — but left unchecked, they become isolation chambers, if not a prison.

In attachment trauma, walls feel safer than vulnerability because they control exposure to emotional risk.

Fearful-Avoidant Insight:

You build emotional walls disguised as "boundaries." You crave connection but guard yourself against disappointment because life has been unkind to you.

Healing focus: Start noticing what your walls are made of — silence, sarcasm, overthinking, withdrawal. Ask yourself: Is this protecting me, or isolating me? You begin to see more clearly that you are getting into your own way.

Dismissive-Avoidant Insight:

Your wall is made of logic and independence. You tell yourself emotions complicate life, when really, they give it depth. And you have no need for emotional depth.

Healing focus: Vulnerability isn't losing control; it's choosing authenticity. Try naming one emotion each day — not to fix it, but to feel it without shame.

Johanna's Reflection:

Walls are not built overnight. They rise brick by brick — every time we're hurt, rejected, or misunderstood. And before you know it, you can barely see how to get out of it.

But love requires visibility. You can't be loved for who you are if you're never seen. So step out of your comfort zone for once.

It's time to peek over your wall. Not all eyes looking back will hurt you. Some will understand you in ways you didn't know were possible and love you in ways you could never imagine.

Self-Reflection Prompt:
- What does your wall look like — emotional silence, busyness, humor, or control?
- Who do you become when you feel safe enough to lower it?

Chapter Five

Trigger Points

It started small — it always did when it came to catching feelings or expressing them.

Demi asks Craig if he'd thought about taking a trip together. Something simple, a weekend getaway, some alone time without the world's demands. Her voice carried a hint of hope she didn't mean to reveal, but it did.

He froze. "I don't really do trips," he said.

Her smile faltered. "You mean you don't do plans."

The room grew quiet.

"I just don't like to rush into things," he said. "You know that."

Demi looked down at her hands. "It's been seven months, Craig. I don't think this is rushing," and she was right, she was tired of him holding back from her.

He sighed, leaning back on the couch. "Why does everything have to be a big deal?" He had to go there.

And there it was — the moment she felt the ground shift beneath her and her heart racing.

Her chest tightened, her voice dropped. "Because I don't want to keep pretending this is nothing."

Craig looked at her like she'd crossed an invisible line. "I never said it was nothing. You're just... taking things too personally."

Her eyes stung. "You mean I'm having feelings."

He stood, running a hand over his jaw. "This—this is exactly what I'm talking about. You get emotional, and suddenly I'm the bad guy."

She flinched. The way he said emotional sounded like *unreasonable*.

He saw her silence as withdrawal. She saw his withdrawal as rejection.

And both were right — in their own ways.

Neither realized they weren't fighting each other. They were fighting their triggers each in their own way.

Later that night, Demi cried quietly in her car, gripping the steering wheel. She told herself she wouldn't reach out, wouldn't apologize this time. But she did — an hour later, because she can't help herself, and she just wants love.

"I'm sorry. I didn't mean to push."

Craig stared at the message for a long time. He didn't know how to reply without feeling blamed. He typed, "It's okay," and left it at that.

Two words. No repair. Just survival. Same old Craig giving little while someone else puts their heart out in the open.

Reflection Section — Understanding Triggers

Triggers are emotional echoes — old wounds disguised as present reactions can trip you up every time. They're not about what's happening *now*; they're about what once made us feel unsafe.

Fearful-Avoidant Insight:
You may interpret withdrawal as rejection because your nervous system is wired for inconsistency.

When connection feels threatened, your panic isn't an overreaction — it's recognition.

Healing focus: Breathe before responding. Ask yourself, "*What is this reminding me of?*" That question turns reaction into reflection.

Dismissive-Avoidant Insight:
You may feel attacked when someone expresses need or emotion. What you experience as "pressure" is often an invitation to intimacy. This is a space you have not allowed yourself to exist in.

Healing focus: Before shutting down, pause and name what you're feeling — *overwhelmed, unprepared, cornered.* Naming gives you power to stay engaged rather than retreat.

Johanna's Reflection:
Triggers don't mean love is broken. They mean healing is asking to happen.

But triggers can't heal in silence — they need awareness, honesty, and gentleness.

When two people's wounds meet, love becomes a mirror. The goal isn't to win the argument — it's to acknowledge the pain that needs to be witnessed and allow the healing to take place in that area.

Self-Reflection Prompt:
- What patterns of reaction do you notice when you feel misunderstood?
- How can you communicate your discomfort without abandoning yourself or the other person?

Chapter Six
The Space Between

The silence started small — a few days without texting, not a word, which felt harmless at first.

Craig told himself he was giving Demi space, but he was lying to himself, as he always did; he was avoiding his emotions once again. Demi told herself he just needed time.

But that silence stretched, and stretched, until it began to feel like its own kind of conversation.

The kind that says I don't know how to reach you anymore.

Demi sat at her kitchen table one night, her phone face down beside a mug of cold tea; she was no longer interested in sipping. She wanted to text him. She wanted to say, 'I miss you,' or 'I don't know what happened,' but the words caught in her throat; she did not dare speak. It was clear that he did not want what she wanted — a strong connection.

Her pride and her pain were locked in a standoff of flashbacks and past rejection playing in her mind like an old movie.

Meanwhile, Craig scrolled through his messages, pausing on her name. He wanted to reach out, too — but guilt and confusion held him back; he had to stay in control.

Every time he thought about calling, he remembered the tension in her eyes that night. He didn't want to disappoint her again or expose his feelings for her.

So he said nothing.

He convinced himself that silence was kindness.

She convinced herself silence was rejection.

And in that space between their misunderstandings, both of them were hurting — quietly, separately, stubbornly, and alone.

Weeks passed before they ran into each other unexpectedly — in a café they both used to go to. The moment felt like déjà vu, but heavier.

"Hey," Demi said softly.

Craig nodded. "Hey."

They stood awkwardly, both unsure of how much of their pain to reveal.

"How've you been?" she asked.

He shrugged. "Busy."

The word hit her like a wall. The same word he always used when things started slipping.

She smiled politely. "I'm glad."

He nodded again, eyes dropping. "You look good."

And there it was — all the emotion that hadn't been said, compressed into small talk, nothing new, just the same old Craig.

After a moment, Demi turned to leave. "Take care, Craig."

He wanted to stop her, to say something real, but his body betrayed him. His chest tightened, throat closing, he would not dare cross that emotional line that allows you to feel.

He watched her go, realizing too late that emotional distance doesn't protect love — it erodes it, something he had been accustomed to creating in his life.

Reflection Section — Learning from the Space Between

The "space" in relationships isn't always abandonment — sometimes it's avoidance dressed as self-preservation.
However, too much space without communication can lead to emotional starvation and the death of connection.

Fearful-Avoidant Insight:
You may interpret distance as punishment. Silence triggers memories of being unseen or forgotten, even if the person pulling away is doing so out of fear, not malice.

Healing focus: Before filling silence with fear, ground yourself in truth. Ask, *What do I know for sure?* — not *What do I fear most?*

Dismissive-Avoidant Insight:
You use distance to regulate feelings of overwhelm. Space feels safe because it gives you a sense of control. But prolonged space creates loneliness that feels safer than closeness — a cycle that confuses safety with emptiness and fear.

Healing focus: Reach out sooner than you feel comfortable. Connection won't kill your freedom — it will redefine it.

Johanna's Reflection:
Love can't breathe without communication and respect. The space between two people can be healing only if it's filled with honesty and accountability.

When you love from a distance out of fear, you don't protect your heart — you teach it to live half-asleep, never trusting anyone.

Love asks for courage, not perfection. Sometimes courage looks like a single text that says, *"I miss you. Can we talk?"*

Self-Reflection Prompt:

- How do you react when silence enters a relationship?
- Does distance make you feel calm — or does it keep you from being seen?

Chapter Seven

Crossroads

The rain poured steadily that night, blurring the city lights into soft gold streaks on the glass window. Demi sat in her car outside Craig's apartment, hands gripping the steering wheel with all of her might, the hum of the engine filling the silence she didn't know how to break, not even in her fear.

She hadn't planned to be there. Demi's mind told her to go home, to protect herself from Craig.

But her heart — the one that had spent weeks aching in the dark — whispered, Go. You need to know, she needed answers.

When he opened the door, the look on his face told her everything. Surprise, guilt, longing — all tangled into one uneasy breath, not to mention his eyes.

"Demi," he said softly, as if her name itself might vanish if he spoke it too loudly. She was in pain and confusion. Once again, love was avoiding her.

"I wasn't sure you'd answer."

"I almost didn't."

They stood there for a beat too long, silence pressing between them again.

Finally, she stepped inside. "We can't keep doing this," she said. "Whatever this is — the running, the silence, the pretending."

Craig nodded, eyes low. "I know. I don't know how to fix it," and he was so right about that.

"You don't fix it by disappearing every time things get real," she said, her voice cracking. "I get scared, too, Craig. But I don't hide behind it."

He flinched, the words hitting the place he'd tried to protect most in his heart.

"I wasn't trying to hurt you," he said. "I just… I didn't know how to be what you needed. Every time you looked at me like I was supposed to save you, I panicked."

"I never asked you to save me," she said quietly. "I asked you to stay."
For the first time, Craig didn't look away; he could not because her words he felt for the first time.

He reached out, fingers grazing her arm. "You don't know what it's like — always feeling like closeness is a trap. Every time someone gets too close, I feel like I'm disappearing."

"And you don't know what it's like," she replied, "to need connection so badly it feels like air — and to love someone who's always holding their breath."

The room went still.

That was the truth between them — the fearful and the dismissive, circling the same pain from opposite sides for the first time.

They sat on the couch, the storm outside echoing the one within.

Craig finally said, "Maybe we keep hurting each other because we're both afraid of losing control."

"Maybe," Demi said. "But what if control isn't what love needs?"
He looked at her then — really looked. "Then what does it need?"

"Safety," she whispered. "And honesty."

He nodded slowly, the weight of her words sinking in. "Then maybe this is our crossroads he whispered, his voice cracking. We either keep hiding from what we fear — or we learn to face it together."

And for the first time, Craig didn't retreat. He took her hand.

"I don't know how," he said. "But I want to try."

Reflection Section — Standing at Your Crossroads

Every relationship reaches a crossroads — the moment when comfort and growth pull in opposite directions.

Fearful-Avoidant Insight:
You long for closeness but fear it will end in pain. At the crossroads, your instinct might be to retreat or test your partner's love.
Healing focus: Stop testing and start trusting. You can't discover safety without risking vulnerability.

Dismissive-Avoidant Insight:
You value independence, but independence without intimacy can lead to isolation. At the crossroads, choosing connection means surrendering control — not your identity.

Healing focus: Let love challenge your walls, not define your worth.

Johanna's Reflection:

Crossroads moments are sacred — they reveal who we truly are when we are under pressure. Love isn't proven by who stays through the easy parts, but by who leans in when everything feels uncertain.

Healing doesn't happen when you find the "right" person — it happens when you become willing to grow with them.

Self-Reflection Prompt:

- What crossroads have you faced in love or friendship?
- Do you tend to retreat or reach out when connection feels risky?
- What would "trying" look like for you right now?

Chapter Eight
The Mirror Work

The next morning, the air between them was different. Not lighter — but realer *something neither had ever experienced.*

Demi sat at Craig's kitchen table, fingers tracing the rim of her mug as sunlight poured across the counter. The city outside was alive again, indifferent to the fragile truce that had formed between them.

She hadn't stayed the night. But she hadn't run, either.

Craig leaned against the counter, quiet, almost gentle. "You ever feel like you don't know who you are when you're in love?" he asked.

Demi looked up. "All the time."

He gave a small smile. "Yeah. Me too."

They sat in that truth — two people realizing that love was not their biggest enemy. It was their *reflection* in it that scared them, but they were embracing it together.

Later that week, Demi began journaling again — something she hadn't done in years. Each entry felt like peeling back a layer of armor.

She wrote about the silence that haunted her after arguments, the fear of being too much, the ache of waiting for a text that never came, and the silent but deafening screams she held within.

But this time, instead of asking, *Why doesn't he love me enough?* she asked, *Why don't I feel sufficient without him?*

Craig, on his end, had started therapy — quietly, without telling her at first. His therapist had asked him something that stuck:

"What does closeness feel like to you — safe or suffocating?"

At first, he said "suffocating." Then after a pause, he added, "But maybe only because I never learned what safe felt like." he was finally seeing who he was when it came to love, a prisoner of his own thoughts.

A few days later, they met again at their favorite café. No plans, no promises — just presence.

"I've been working on something," Craig said.

Demi arched a brow. "What kind of something?"

He pulled out a small notebook, its edges worn. Inside were short reflections — confessions, almost.

"I started writing down what happens when I pull away," he said. "Like, the exact thought before I disappear. I noticed it's always the same story."

"What story?"

"That I'm about to lose myself. That if I let you all the way in, I'll vanish."

Demi nodded, tears gathering. "I've been writing too. But for me, it's the opposite — I start to believe that if you pull away, I'm not worth staying for." That confession hit harder than either realized.

They sat there, realizing how their fears fed each other. His withdrawal confirmed her abandonment. Her pursuit confirmed his fear of being trapped.

They had both been looking in a mirror, but mistaking each other's reflection for the enemy.

That night, Demi wrote:

"Healing doesn't happen when he changes. It happens when I stop letting fear drive my love."

And Craig wrote:

"She's not my mirror — she's my teacher. But the lesson starts with me."

Reflection Section — The Mirror Within

The mirror work is about recognizing that relationships *reflect* our beliefs about love and ourselves, as well as the hard truths we often stuff deep down within. They don't create our wounds — they reveal them.

Fearful-Avoidant Insight:

You often fear rejection while unconsciously recreating it. When love feels uncertain, your instinct to cling or overanalyze is an attempt to control what you can't soothe within.

Healing focus: Learn to self-soothe. Emotional regulation is self-love in motion.

Dismissive-Avoidant Insight:

You fear being consumed by someone's needs, so you detach before intimacy deepens. The distance protects your independence — but also isolates you from connection.

Healing focus: Practice staying present in discomfort. Connection doesn't erase you — it expands you.

Johanna's Reflection:

We attract what will show us what still needs healing. Each relationship, whether peaceful or painful, is a mirror of our readiness for truth in exchange for a genuine connection, and it's not to break us but to grow us up.
Healing isn't about blaming your reflection — it's about loving yourself enough to *see clearly and make changes that will better your life as well as find true love or friendship.*

Self-Reflection Prompt:

- What recurring pattern shows up in your relationships?
- When triggered, do you reach for connection or retreat into silence?
- How can you start mirroring love instead of fear in your daily interactions?

Chapter Nine
The Reconnection

It had been three weeks since Demi and Craig had spoken.

Three weeks of silence that hummed with everything left unsaid.

But healing wasn't always loud—it sometimes whispered through small changes that are often overlooked.

For Demi, it looked like morning walks, rather than checking her phone every few minutes.

For Craig, it was learning to breathe through discomfort rather than escape it.

When they finally saw each other again, it was not planned; they somehow ended up in the same place.

It was a chance encounter—one of those city collisions that feel like fate's gentle nudge, you know the ones you can't avoid.

Demi was leaving her therapy session; Craig was grabbing a coffee from the shop below.

Their eyes met as if it was the first time, and time for a moment stood stilled just long enough for both to remember what connection *used to feel like.*

"Hey," she said softly.

Craig smiled, a bit hesitant. "Hey. You look... grounded," he said with a half smile.

"Trying to be," she whispered with a smile.

They stood in awkward warmth, both unsure of how to move forward but unwilling to walk away again. More needed to be said, but the awkwardness was loud.

Later that evening, they met at the pier where they had once watched the city lights reflect over the water.

This time, there were no grand gestures from either of them. No apologies rehearsed, something they would always do.

Just truth something long overdue.

"I've been doing the work," Craig said quietly, his gaze fixed on the skyline. "Therapy. Journaling. Sitting with the things I used to avoid."

Demi nodded. "I can tell."

He turned to her then, eyes softer than she remembered. "And you? What's changed?"

"I stopped distancing myself from my worth," she smiled faintly. "That's new for me."

He exhaled, the weight of years of pattern loosening just a little. "You always deserved better than my fear."

"And you always deserved more than my need for constant reassurance," she replied.

The honesty between them was quiet, not forced. For once, love wasn't a battlefield—it was a conversation, and you could tell by Demi's eyes that she had noticed a difference in Craig.

As they walked, Craig reached for her hand. It wasn't a claim. It was an invitation.

Demi hesitated for a moment, then intertwined her fingers with his.

It felt different—steady, not desperate. Present, not perfumed with fear.

"I'm not promising I won't struggle," he said, voice low and clear. "But I want to stay through the struggle, no matter how long it takes."

"That's all I ever wanted," Demi whispered, as her eyes turned from looking at the skyline and into Craig's eyes.

For the first time, their silence felt like a connection rather than distance, and for Demi, this feeling was good.

That night, Demi wrote in her journal:

"We're not who we were when this started. We're learning to meet each other halfway—not out of fear, but out of awareness. This is what reconnection feels like."

And Craig's note from his therapist session read:

"Reconnection isn't about returning to the past—it's about creating a new way to be close while respecting boundaries."

Reflection Section — The Reconnection Within

Healing in avoidant dynamics often requires redefining what *connection* means since everyone has their own interpretation of healing.

It's not about constant closeness—it's about *safe consistency and honesty.*

Fearful-Avoidant Insight:

You crave connection but fear rejection because you have been hurt so much that you protect yourself from the world. When distance appears, you interpret it as a sign of abandonment.

Healing focus: Develop emotional independence so that connection becomes a choice, not a necessity.

Dismissive-Avoidant Insight:
You protect your autonomy by keeping love at arm's length. Yet, true freedom is found in relationships where you can *be yourself without retreating.*

Healing focus: Practice taking small emotional risks—share a truth, admit a need, and stay present during discomfort.

Johanna's Reflection:
Reconnection doesn't mean starting over. It means coming back *as your healed self and being true to yourself and those you care about.*

In love, we are not meant to complete each other—but to *witness* one another's growth.

Self-Reflection Prompts:

- What does safety in connection feel like to you—peaceful or restricting?
- How do you know when reconnection is genuine, not born of fear or loneliness?
- What new boundaries or behaviors would reflect your healed self in love?

Chapter Ten

Love in Real Time

The morning sunlight streamed through Demi's kitchen window, illuminating the steam rising from two mugs of coffee.

Craig sat at the table, barefoot, reading the morning news on his phone. It should have felt like an ordinary moment, but for them, *ordinary* was something new.

After weeks of cautious reconnection, they were now trying to live their love out loud — not just talk about it or analyze it — but *experience it like* never before.

Demi stirred sugar into her cup, watching him. "You seem calm today," she said.

He smiled, almost shy. "I am. I didn't check out before coming over."

She laughed softly. "That's progress."

It was progress — the kind that didn't look dramatic but felt deeply earned.

Before, Craig's nervous system would spike with anxiety at the slightest sign of emotional closeness; he had permitted himself to exist in the moment.

Now, he could sit in the presence of love without wanting to flee.

And Demi? She was learning to stop scanning for danger for the first time in her life. She wasn't waiting for rejection anymore; she had learned to love herself above all if you want to flourish in love.

Later that afternoon, they walked through the park. Children's laughter echoed around them; the air carried the scent of cut grass and distant food trucks.

"I used to think love was supposed to fix me," Demi said suddenly.

Craig nodded, eyes thoughtful. "I used to think love was supposed to leave me alone."

They both laughed — because it was true. And because laughing together was a kind of healing, and it was something they desperately needed.

He reached for her hand, not to claim, but to connect. She didn't pull away this time.

"Love in real time," she murmured. "Messy, human, and kind."

That night, after Craig left, Demi wrote another journal entry:

"I didn't need him to be perfect today. I needed him to *be present, and he was.* Maybe that's what healing love looks like — two people choosing awareness over fear, moment by moment."

Craig wrote in his notes:

"For the first time, I didn't feel like I had to protect myself from love. I let it happen, and nothing bad came of it. Maybe it's not the world that needs to change — maybe it's how I meet it," he said while staring at his journal notes.

Reflection Section — Staying Present in Love

Love isn't a concept to master; it's a practice to live *in real time.*

For avoidant types, staying emotionally present is one of the hardest — and most transformative — acts of healing.

Fearful-Avoidant Insight:

You oscillate between craving closeness and fearing rejection. When love feels too good, you start bracing for loss.

Healing focus: Practice noticing safety in the present. Ask yourself, "*Am I safe right now*?" and anchor into that moment.

Dismissive-Avoidant Insight:
You often equate intimacy with a loss of control. Yet true intimacy is not engulfing — it's *a shared* autonomy.

Healing focus: Let love be an equal exchange. Please stay in the conversation even when it feels uncomfortable.

Johanna's Reflection:

Real love doesn't ask you to erase your defenses overnight or trust without question. It asks you to *notice them* and choose something softer, like a healthier way of communicating without fear.

To love in real time is to accept that healing is not a straight line — it's a rhythm, a dance between fear and courage, and that dance can move in circles, a straight line, or in random directions. Keep up.

Self-Reflection Prompts:

- What does "being present" mean in your relationships?
- When do you notice yourself checking out emotionally — and why?
- How might you remind yourself that love and safety can coexist?

Chapter Eleven
Triggers and Truths

The rain came without warning.

Demi stood by her window, watching droplets race each other down the glass. Craig was late—again.

It wasn't just the lateness. It was the silence that came with it. No call. No text.

Old fears rose fast, like reflex within Demi.

He's pulling away.

You've said too much.

He's done with you, her thoughts raced through her mind.

Demi's mind spiraled into that familiar anxious loop—the one that used to control her.

When the knock finally came, she had already rehearsed her retreat—short answers, cold tone, guarded stance.

Craig stepped in, soaked from the rain. "I'm sorry. The meeting ran long, and my phone died. I should've let you know sooner."

Demi crossed her arms. "You think?" Her voice came out sharper than she intended.

Craig's jaw tightened. He hated this tone—it sounded like blame, and blame always felt like rejection.

"I said I'm sorry, Demi. I'm here now, aren't I?"

The air thickened—two nervous systems in survival mode, colliding head-on, just like old times.

For a long moment, neither spoke.

Demi took a slow breath, feeling her heart hammer. *Don't run. Don't spiral.*

"I know," she finally said. "You're here. It just brought up old stuff. Being left waiting."

That softened something in him.

"I get that. When you sounded angry, it made me want to shut down. Like, no matter what I said, it wouldn't be enough."

They stood in the raw truth of it—two avoidant hearts learning to speak instead of retreat.

Later, they sat on the couch, the rain still tapping at the windows.

Craig brushed his thumb over her hand. "We did better this time."

Demi smiled faintly. "We didn't run." She was feeling good about everything for the first time.

They laughed softly, the tension dissolving into something almost tender, a place in their connection they had never experienced until this moment.

That night, Demi wrote:

"Triggers don't mean failure. They mean there's still something to understand and work on. Today, we faced it instead of fleeing it."

Craig's reflection from therapy read:

"Truth is what turns triggers into tools. You can't heal what you keep hiding from." Open eyes bring truth in different ways. When you are ready for change, you will see it.

Reflection Section — Turning Triggers into Truths

Triggers are the body's memory of danger. They aren't the enemy—they're a message: *something still needs care.*

For avoidant types, triggers usually lead to withdrawal, shutdown, or overthinking. But healing starts when you pause and name what's really happening. This is when you make the connection to how you have been holding yourself back.

Fearful-Avoidant Insight:

You might interpret delayed communication or silence as rejection, but it is not.

Healing focus: Instead of reacting, ask yourself, *"What story am I telling myself right now?"*

Truth interrupts the fear narrative.

Dismissive-Avoidant Insight:
You often shut down to avoid emotional overwhelm or perceived criticism.

Healing focus: Stay curious instead of defensive.

Ask, "What is my partner really needing right now?"

Johanna's Reflection:

Triggers are opportunities disguised as discomfort. They show you where love still feels unsafe—and where healing wants to enter.

When you stay present long enough to find the truth behind your fear, connection deepens. That's where real intimacy begins. You begin to feel untouched by the past, brand new in an old world, and that feeling is refreshing not just for you but for all whom you connect with.

Self-Reflection Prompts:

- What situations trigger your urge to pull away or overreact?
- How do you usually protect yourself when you feel unseen or criticized?
- Can you practice curiosity instead of controlling the next time you're triggered?

Chapter Twelve
Safe Space

The city was softer that evening — rain-slick streets reflecting light like melted gold. Demi's apartment smelled of sage and sandalwood — a calm space she had intentionally created.

Craig sat cross-legged on the floor beside her, both of them wrapped in quiet that didn't feel heavy anymore or forced. The silence between them had changed — it was no longer a wall; it was a space to breathe and let their guard down.

Demi took a slow sip of her warm tea. "You know what's weird?" she said finally. "For the first time, I don't feel like I have to *earn* peace."

Craig looked up, curious. "What do you mean?"

"I used to think I had to be perfect or easy to love. If I hadn't made a mistake, I could have avoided conflict. But this..." She gestured between them; she had no fear telling her truth for the first time, and it felt good. "This peace feels mutual. Safe."

He nodded, smiling gently. "That's because we're not performing anymore. We are operating in our truth."

She let out a laugh, soft and true. "You're right. We're just being." For the first time, they were free from fear and free to express their feelings.

Later that night, they played a card game she found online — *36 Questions to Build Emotional Intimacy*.

At first, it felt silly. Then, unexpectedly real.

"What's your biggest fear in love?" Demi read aloud.

Craig hesitated, looking down at his hands. "That I'll disappoint someone so much they leave."

She nodded, voice quiet. "I used to fear that too. Except mine was the other side of that — that I'd be too much and make someone leave."

Their eyes met. The honesty didn't hurt this time. It healed, and they both felt that healing taking place.

"That's the irony," Craig murmured. "Both of us are afraid of being left, just for different reasons." The realist thing he's ever said, and it was out loud.

By the end of the game, the air between them was thick with understanding — not tension.

Demi leaned against him, her head on his shoulder.

"I think we just made a safe space," she said softly.

He smiled. "No, *we remembered* how to create one."

That night, Demi journaled:

"Safety isn't the absence of fear or love. It's the presence of care. We didn't avoid pain tonight — we faced it together, and that made it safe."

Craig's therapy notes read:

"Emotional safety means being honest without being punished. It's not about perfection — it's about permission."

Reflection Section — Building a Safe Space in Love
Safety is the foundation of secure attachment. Without it, love becomes survival.

To love as a healed person means making space for honesty, softness, and acknowledging mistakes.

Fearful-Avoidant Insight:

You may equate safety with control — trying to manage outcomes to avoid rejection.

Healing focus: Let others show you they can handle your truth. Safety grows when you *allow* rather than *protect*.

Dismissive-Avoidant Insight:
You may confuse independence with safety, believing distance equals peace.

Healing focus: Learn that safety can exist *with* connection, not only in solitude.

Johanna's Reflection:

Safe love doesn't mean conflict never happens — it means both people know how to return to a calm state of mind.
Safety is built through consistency, accountability, and compassion — not perfection.

Self-Reflection Prompts:
What does emotional safety feel like in your body?
How do you currently protect your peace — by withdrawal, or by communication?
How can you practice creating safety in your next honest conversation?

Chapter Thirteen

Old Wounds, New Patterns

The argument started over something small — a half-read message on Craig's phone.

Demi saw it, froze, and her chest tightened like old times. Not because she thought he was unfaithful, but because *the silence afterward* felt familiar.

It echoed old pain, the kind that whispered, Y*ou're about to be left again.*

She didn't lash out this time. She didn't retreat. She just… shut down, unsure what to feel or say.

Craig noticed immediately.

"What just happened?" he asked gently.

"Nothing," she said, her voice flat. "It's fine," she said, in deep thought.

He sighed. "That's your 'I'm scared but pretending not to be' voice."

Her eyes flicked up, surprised. He'd noticed, and it shocked her.

"Talk to me," he said softly.

She hesitated. The old version of her would've armored up, blamed him, or ghosted herself emotionally, and she wanted to rush out the door, but did not.

Instead, she exhaled. "It's not about the message. It's just… my brain went back. When people stopped choosing me without explanation, it's old stuff."

Craig nodded. "Yeah. Old stuff sneaks in like that."

He paused, choosing his words carefully. "When you went quiet, my first instinct was to defend myself. Then I realized, that's my old stuff — thinking I'm being attacked when I'm really being needed."

Their eyes met, and both smiled — a weary, knowing kind of smile, but they were facing their fears and truth all at the same time, and you could see it.

That evening, they sat together on the couch, both journaling silently — a ritual they'd started whenever triggers appeared.

It wasn't about solving anything immediately. It was about staying open long enough to *see* the pattern before repeating it; this was the only proper way to take control and change your actions and behaviors.

Demi's pen moved slowly across the page:

"My wound tells me I have to earn love. My healing reminds me I already deserve it."

Craig wrote:

"My wound tells me I need distance to stay safe. My healing reminds me closeness can be safety, too."

They looked up at each other and laughed softly. "We're getting good at this," Demi said.

Craig chuckled. "Practice makes patterns."

That night, for the first time in years, they fell asleep without emotional residue between them — no silent wars, no hidden fear— just quiet understanding.

Reflection Section — Healing Old Wounds with New Patterns

Healing means bringing awareness to the old emotional scripts you inherited — the fears, defenses, and coping behaviors that once protected you but now prevent intimacy.

Fearful-Avoidant Insight:
You often replay abandonment patterns, believing safety must be earned.

Healing focus: Notice when you start bracing for loss. Ground yourself in present safety — what's true right now.

Dismissive-Avoidant Insight:
You may mistake emotional independence for strength, avoiding vulnerability to prevent being controlled.

Healing focus: Let yourself be seen in small, consistent ways. Sharing feelings doesn't reduce freedom — it deepens trust.

Johanna's Reflection:
Old wounds don't disappear just because you understand them. They soften when you respond differently. Each time you choose patience over panic or honesty over avoidance, you teach your nervous system a new love story —one that says, 'I am here forever.'

Self-Reflection Prompts:

- What old stories about love or safety still shape how you react?
- How can you tell when an old wound is running your current response?
- How can you tell if your bruised heart is pushing you to shut down?
- What new pattern could you create to rewrite that emotional script?

Chapter Fourteen
Relearning Intimacy

The night felt heavy with unspoken things, but neither one left. They faced their fears. Demi sat cross-legged on the bed, a blanket around her shoulders, while Craig leaned against the doorframe, quiet but present. He promised himself not to run away from Demi, made that same promise, even though no one said a word.

"I didn't grow up seeing love like this," Demi said finally. "When people got close, something bad usually followed. Silence. Anger. Leaving."

Craig nodded slowly. "Same. I learned that distance brings peace and that you should never let that person back into your life. But I guess peace built on distance isn't really peace — it's avoidance." Another truth that hit home.

She smiled faintly. "So what do we do now?"

He walked closer, sitting beside her. "Maybe we start by unlearning what we thought intimacy was supposed to look like."

Unlearning the Old Definitions
For years, intimacy for Demi meant *anticipation* — always watching for the next emotional shift. For Craig, it meant *control* — keeping feelings at arm's length so he wouldn't get lost in them.

Now, both were discovering a gentler kind: *safety in the present moment.*

They tried something new: quiet touch without an agenda. No fixing, no testing. Just a connection. They were all in and ready for what was to come. They did not struggle with their fears alone; for the first time, they had each other to support them.

As Demi rested her head on Craig's shoulder, her mind started to run — *What if this ends? What if he gets tired of needing reassurance from me?*

But instead of pulling away, she named it.

"My brain's trying to sabotage this," she whispered, and boy was she so right. Speaking out loud was the best thing she could have done.

Craig chuckled softly. "Mine too. It says I should be doing something, solving something. Just sitting here feels too still."

She smiled. "Then let's just sit still together."

Practice Makes Presence
They began weaving new rituals into their relationship — small, grounding acts of connection that didn't rely on drama or defense. Talk about a power move, this was it.

Morning check-ins instead of morning silence.

Honest pauses instead of avoidance.

A hand squeeze to say *I'm here* when words felt too heavy.

It wasn't perfect. There were slips — moments when Craig retreated behind sarcasm, or Demi over-explained her feelings to prove worthiness. But they caught themselves faster each time, and that was all that mattered. There was no need to change.

Healing wasn't about being flawless; it was about being *aware* and choosing gentleness anyway.

That weekend, Demi looked at Craig and said, "You know, I used to think love meant never being scared. But now I see it's being scared and staying open anyway." And he was right because it was the only way to get through the fear of rejection.

He took her hand. "And I used to think love meant not needing anyone. But maybe it's about needing each other, honestly." Finally, he's got it right.

Reflection Section — The Art of Relearning Intimacy

Relearning intimacy means creating safety *in connection* rather than *through distance.* It's letting your body experience closeness as calm, not chaos.

Fearful-Avoidant Insight:

You may crave closeness but fear it once it arrives.

Healing focus: Learn to tolerate emotional presence. Breathe through the discomfort of being seen without shrinking.

Dismissive-Avoidant Insight:
You may equate self-sufficiency with safety, pulling back when emotions rise.

Healing focus: Allow yourself to *need.* Interdependence isn't weakness; it's mature love in motion.

Johanna's Reflection:

Intimacy isn't built in grand gestures — it's sustained in micro-moments of truth. When you let someone see your unfinished parts and they stay, the nervous system begins to believe that love doesn't have to hurt to be real.

Self-Reflection Prompts:

- What does intimacy feel like in your body — safety, fear, control, peace?
- When you feel the urge to withdraw or overreact, what emotion is beneath it?
- How can you build rituals of closeness that don't depend on perfection, but presence?

Chapter Fifteen
The Setback

The weekend started with fun and laughter.

Music played low, sunlight filtered through the curtains, and for once, Demi and Craig felt steady — like maybe all the hard work was finally paying off. They were happy, and it showed on their faces.

However, healing doesn't progress in a straight line. It circles back, testing what's been learned like a washing machine going from soaking to spin overnight.

It happened over something small — a forgotten text, a delay in reply. Demi felt that old, familiar panic rise: *He's drifting again. She gave him no room for error.*

She tried to push it down, but her silence stretched into something sharp, something she could not ignore.

When Craig came home, the air was already charged.

"You could've just said you were busy," she blurted out, and just like that, she welcomed back her old fears.

Craig stiffened. "I didn't think I needed to check in every few hours."

There it was — the trigger point dressed as logic. And so he defended his position.

Demi crossed her arms. "You don't get it. You disappear, and I spiral."

He exhaled through his nose, fighting to stay calm. "And when I feel cornered, I shut down. We both know this dance." At this moment, they were both operating out of fear, but they were talking.

Old Patterns, New Awareness

They didn't yell this time. They just stared — two people aware of their patterns but still caught in them.

Craig sat down on the couch. "I hate that you think I'm pulling away. It's not that simple."

"I hate that I still get scared every time there's space," Demi admitted. "Even after all this work."

He looked up. "Maybe this is the work — catching ourselves mid-pattern instead of pretending we're past it." Yes! He was telling the truth; they could not deny it.

For the first time, they didn't run from the setback. They sat in it.

Not to fix it. To feel it. It did not feel good; it brought back the scary feelings, the hurt, and pain, and they allowed themselves to feel it, no matter how uncomfortable it felt.

The Anatomy of a Setback

Healing doesn't mean never slipping. It means responding to the slip in a different way.

When Craig withdrew, Demi didn't chase as far.

When Demi spiraled, Craig didn't vanish for days.

They now had enough awareness to pause, breathe, and return to the middle.

Later that night, Craig placed his phone face down and said quietly, "I don't want to go back to surviving love. I want to build it."

Demi smiled, tearful but calm. "Then let's build slow."

Reflection Section — Understanding Setbacks

Setbacks aren't proof of failure. They're *data*.

Each emotional regression reveals where the wound still resides, calling for care rather than correction.

Fearful-Avoidant Insight:
You may equate emotional tension with danger, causing you to panic or cling when things feel uncertain.

Healing focus: Pause before acting. Name what you feel — fear, shame, abandonment — without assigning blame. This gives you back your power and allows you to grow in love. They were doing the work and seeing the results.

Dismissive-Avoidant Insight:

You may interpret conflict as a threat to autonomy and withdraw to protect yourself.

Healing focus: Re-engage slowly. Offer reassurance, not retreat. Your presence repairs what silence once broke.

Johanna's Reflection:

Every relationship faces storms. The goal isn't to avoid them, but to weather them differently.

When love becomes safe enough to handle rupture and repair, that's when it begins to mature.

Self-Reflection Prompts:

- When I experience conflict, do I rush toward control or retreat into distance?
- What does my nervous system need in the middle of emotional rupture — space, words, or touch?
- How do I define "progress" in healing — perfection, or the ability to come back together faster each time?

Chapter Sixteen
The Repair Ritual

A New Way to Begin Again

They sat on the couch, side by side but not touching, not this time.

"I don't want to rehash what we said," Craig began. "I want to understand how we both got there."

Demi nodded. "Okay. I'll go first."

Her voice trembled at first, but she didn't hold back.

"When I don't hear from you, my mind goes to worst-case scenarios. I start to believe I'm not important — that you're slipping away."

Craig listened, eyes steady, body language open — something he'd never been good at before.

He said, "When you come at me with that fear, I freeze. It's not because I don't care. It's because I don't know how to handle feeling needed that much."

They paused for a moment.

No one defended.

No one blamed.

Just two people speaking truth instead of fear.

The Ritual of Repair

They didn't call it that, but that's what it became — a *ritual*.

Whenever tension rose, they followed the same steps:

1. **Pause before reacting.** They agreed to wait at least twenty minutes before engaging after a fight. This is powerful because it allows them to control the following steps, move, and how they wish to make the other feel.
2. **Name the wound, not the weapon.** Instead of "You ignored me," Demi said, "I felt unseen." Communication is key in any relationship, and how you express yourself can significantly aid in its growth.
3. **Own your part. Craig learned to admit,** "I pulled away," instead of pretending nothing was wrong. Craig shows that he was growing and not afraid to express his feelings.
4. **Reconnect through small gestures.** A hand on the shoulder, a quiet "I'm still here," replaced long silences. It allows your relationship to continue the healing.

The ritual wasn't about pretending nothing hurt.

It was about proving the relationship could *survive the hurt.*

Later that evening, Demi whispered, "I used to think love was only safe when it was easy."

Craig smiled faintly. "Turns out, it's only real when we repair what breaks." And he was right.

Reflection Section — Building a Repair Ritual

Conflict isn't the enemy. *Disconnection without repair is.*

A repair ritual creates a framework — a way back home when emotional storms hit.

It transforms moments of rupture into opportunities for deeper intimacy.

For Fearful-Avoidant Healing:

You may equate distance with abandonment. Instead of rushing to reconnect through panic, take a moment to soothe your nervous system first.
Try saying: "I'm feeling scared right now, but I still want to work this out."

For Dismissive-Avoidant Healing:

You may associate closeness with losing control. Challenge yourself to stay present even when it's uncomfortable because this is how you repair your relationship.

Try saying: "I need a moment, but I'm not leaving this conversation."

Johanna's Reflection:

Repair is love's proof. It's the quiet, consistent return that builds safety and trust. It's how your love flourishes.
When you can argue and still choose connection, you've begun to heal not just the relationship, but your attachment wounds, and that is how you win.

Self-Reflection Prompts:

- What personal "repair ritual" can I create to navigate emotional ruptures more consciously?
- How do I typically respond after conflict — by closing off or reaching out?
- When have I felt most loved after a disagreement? What made that moment feel safe?

Chapter Seventeen
The Vulnerability Pact

The night was quiet except for the hum of the city outside their window.

Craig leaned against the kitchen counter, scrolling through his phone but not really reading anything. Demi sat on the couch, curled up, replaying their last conversation in her head. It hadn't been a fight this time—just... avoidance. The kind of silence that grows when both people are too scared to speak first.

Finally, Demi said, softly but clearly, what was on her mind, "Can I ask you something without you shutting down?"
Craig looked up, cautious. "Yeah. Go ahead."

She hesitated. "Do you ever feel like we're both still hiding?"

The question lingered like smoke. Craig set his phone down to make sure he heard everything Demi was saying.

"I think I've spent most of my life hiding," Craig admitted. "Even from myself."

Demi nodded. "Me too." I never want to hide again, Craig admitted.

Breaking the Pattern

They moved to the floor, sitting cross-legged across from each other—no distractions, just raw honesty.

Demi reached for a notebook, flipping it open.

"I've been reading about emotional safety. They said vulnerability isn't about dumping everything—it's about showing up, even when it's hard."

Craig exhaled. "That sounds terrifying."

"It is," she said with a small laugh. "But maybe we can make it less scary. Like a pact." This was a great way to correct that fear and rejection, followed by saying things that hurt the other person.

Craig tilted in \his head. "A vulnerability pact?"

She smiled. "Exactly." This was a great idea and it meant Craig understood her feelings.

The Pact

Together, they started listing what vulnerability could look like between them. Not grand confessions, but small, everyday risks that built trust.

Their Vulnerability Pact:
1. **No pretending.** If something hurts, they name it instead of swallowing it.
2. **No disappearing.** When things get uncomfortable, they agree to stay emotionally present.
3. **No mind-reading. They ask, instead of assuming.**
4. **No punishment for honesty.** Whatever truth is shared, it's received with curiosity, not criticism.
5. **One small truth a day.** Each day, they share one thing they might usually keep hidden—a fear, a thought, a memory.

When they finished writing, Demi looked up, eyes glassy.

"Do you realize what this means?" she whispered.

Craig nodded. "We're building something new."

He took her hand. "You first."

Demi swallowed hard. "I'm scared you'll see how much I need you."

Craig squeezed her fingers gently. "Then I'll tell you something too—I'm scared, I don't know how to be needed without running."

They both laughed through the tears, the kind that come when you finally exhale after years of holding your breath.

Reflection Section — The Courage to Be Seen

Vulnerability isn't just about honesty. It's about **emotional exposure with safety**—showing your authentic self without fear of rejection.

For Fearful-Avoidant Healing:

You often crave closeness but fear it will lead to loss. Start with micro-vulnerabilities—tiny truths you can share safely. Let your nervous system learn that openness doesn't always lead to pain.

For Dismissive-Avoidant Healing:

You may see vulnerability as weakness. But real strength lies in being able to say, "I need you," and still feel whole. You don't lose power by being open—you gain connection.

Johanna's Reflection:

Vulnerability is the bridge that turns love into safety. It's the quiet, trembling truth that says, *I want you to see me, even if it's uncomfortable.*

When two people can reveal their hidden selves without running, healing begins. These changes, no matter how small or significant, aid in the healing process and strengthen your connection.

Self-Reflection Prompts:

- What does vulnerability mean to you? How has it felt unsafe in the past?
- What's one truth I've been afraid to share in my relationships?
- How can I start building my own "vulnerability pact" with someone I trust—or with myself?

Chapter Eighteen
The Secure Space

Mornings felt different now.

There was still coffee, still the quiet hum of the city, but the silence between them no longer carried tension — it carried ease.

Craig sat by the window, reading, while Demi scribbled in her journal—no one needed to fill the space with words. The quiet had become... safe.

It had been months since they made the Vulnerability Pact. They didn't always get it right — there were still triggers, minor misunderstandings — but recovery came faster now. Fear no longer dictated their rhythm; love did.

Demi closed her journal and looked at Craig. "You know what's strange?" she said.

He looked up. "What?"

"I don't wake up scared anymore. I used to check for signs you were pulling away before I even got out of bed."

Craig smiled faintly. "I used to wake up trying to figure out how much space I could keep without losing you."

They both laughed — softly, knowingly. This was growth. This was grace, and most of all, the connection was stronger.

The Feeling of Safety

Later that evening, they cooked dinner together and shared a laugh. Music played softly in the background, the air filled with the scent of garlic and warmth.

At one point, Craig reached for a pan, accidentally bumping Demi's arm.

She looked at him — a quick flash of the old reaction, the instinct to withdraw — but instead, she smiled.

"It's okay," she said gently. "I know you didn't mean it."

Craig paused, realizing how small moments like this used to spiral into days of silence. He was realizing how he had overreacted and missed the loving connection in the past, but today he was all in.

Now, one gentle acknowledgment diffused everything.

He leaned closer. "You know what this feels like?"

"What?"

"Home," he said. This was beautiful; love was in the air.

Secure Doesn't Mean Perfect

That night, as they lay together, Demi whispered, "Do you think it'll always be this easy?" What she was feeling felt to good to be true.

Craig chuckled softly. "Probably not. But I think we finally know what to do when it's not."

She nodded, pressing closer.

The truth was, safety didn't mean the absence of pain — it meant trust in the process. They had learned how to turn toward each other, even when it hurt.

For the first time, love didn't feel like walking on glass.

It felt like standing barefoot on solid ground.

Reflection Section — Cultivating a Secure Space

A secure space isn't a place; it's an energy you co-create — one where both people can show up fully, without fear of rejection or control.

For Fearful-Avoidant Healing:

You've learned to expect instability so that safety may feel unfamiliar. Let it.
Notice when peace feels "boring." That's not disconnection — it's calm. Your body is learning to rest.

For Dismissive-Avoidant Healing:
You've built protection through independence. Allow safety to mean *interdependence* — not losing yourself, but sharing yourself willingly. Learn that closeness can coexist with freedom and without fear. It all comes down to facing your fears and owning your truths.

Johanna's Reflection:

A secure bond isn't born from perfection — it's built through consistent repair, openness, and empathy.
When two people learn that love can survive truth, they begin to rewrite the story of attachment itself. They become the person opposite of their past fears, insecurities, and vulnerabilities. A healthier person emerges from the trauma.

And that is a stable, secure, and available person who appears more assertive and more confident than they were.

Self-Reflection Prompts:

- What does emotional safety feel like in my body?
- How can I communicate my needs without fear of rejection?
- What does it mean to me to "feel at home" in a relationship?

Chapter Nineteen
Integration

The seasons had shifted again. Leaves brushed the sidewalk outside the apartment, and sunlight spilled softly through half-open blinds across the room.

Craig stirred his coffee slowly, watching as the swirl of cream dissolved and the sunlight spread across the room. He wasn't anxious anymore—not about Demi leaving, not about saying the wrong thing. The stillness he felt wasn't foreign now; it was earned. He had put in the work, and Demi also.

Demi came out of the bedroom, her notebook tucked under her arm. She kissed the top of his head before sitting beside him.

"Guess what?" she said with a grin.

"What?"

"I read something this morning that said healing isn't about becoming someone new. It's about remembering who you were before the fear."

Craig smiled. "I think that's what we've been doing all along."

She nodded. "Integrating."

Two Journeys, One Path

There was no big moment of arrival, no cinematic epiphany—just the soft unfolding of two people who had finally learned to be gentle with themselves.

They'd both done the inner work separately—Demi through journaling and therapy, and Craig through mindfulness and hard self-reflection—but now, integration meant something different.

It meant:

- Bringing self-awareness into their relationship.
- Recognizing triggers without spiraling.
- Holding space for difference without fear.

When Craig got quiet, Demi no longer assumed he was withdrawing. She'd ask, *"Are you taking a moment or checking out?"*

And Craig would answer honestly.

When Demi's voice rose, Craig no longer heard accusation; he heard pain. He'd place his hand on her knee and say, *"I'm listening."*

Each time they practiced awareness instead of reaction, they reinforced the new pattern.

The Everyday Wholeness

That weekend, they took a walk through the park where they'd first reconnected. There were no grand declarations, no promises—just steps—steady, shared, grounded.

"Do you ever miss the old version of us?" Demi asked, half smiling.

Craig shook his head. "No. I think that version got us here. But I don't miss the chaos."

She nodded thoughtfully. "I used to think passion was supposed to hurt."

He smiled. "Now I think peace is the new passion."

They both laughed—because it was true.

Integration wasn't fireworks. It was the quiet joy of knowing that the love they'd fought for now felt natural.

Reflection Section — What Integration Really Means

Integration is the final phase of healing—the moment when emotional awareness becomes instinct.

It's no longer about constantly fixing yourself; it's about *living* as your healed self.

For Fearful-Avoidant Healing:

Integration means realizing that closeness doesn't erase independence. You can be emotionally connected *and* autonomous. Safety no longer feels like waiting for rejection—it feels like staying open even when love is calm.

For Dismissive-Avoidant Healing:

Integration is learning that vulnerability doesn't drain you—it sustains you. True strength lies in the ability not to pull away out of fear.

Johanna's Reflection:

Healing isn't a straight line—it's a spiral. Each time you face an old pattern and respond differently, you integrate another piece of yourself.

That's what Craig and Demi discovered: safety isn't given; it's created, practiced, and embodied. And they were putting in the work to better themselves and their connection. Love does not happen overnight when you are dealing with past trauma, so take your time.

Self-Reflection Prompts:

- How do I know when I've truly integrated my healing, rather than just understanding it?
- What daily habits can I do to help me feel emotionally balanced and grounded in my connections?
- How can I maintain emotional safety while staying open to growth and change?
- How can I make changes more quickly without reverting to a place where I operate out of fear instead of love?

Chapter Twenty
Full Circle

The same café where they first met still smelled of cinnamon and espresso.

It had been two years since that awkward first encounter—two years since two avoidant souls brushed past each other, both unaware of the healing that would follow.

Craig arrived first this time. He sat by the window, the city alive outside but quiet within him. When Demi walked in, his chest didn't tighten like it used to; it expanded. He was relaxed.

She spotted him and smiled—the kind of smile that said *I see you, and I know you see me too.*

Craig stood, pulled her into an embrace, and for a moment, they just breathed each other in. No words, no analysis, no fear. Just presence. Everything they had done up to this point was worth the peace and happiness they shared.

Returning as New Versions of Themselves

They talked about everything and nothing—how work was going, how much they'd grown, how it felt to be back here.

"It's strange," Demi said, tracing the rim of her mug. "This place used to make me anxious." Now she was at peace, and it reflected across her face.

"Why?" Craig asked, though he already knew. He just wanted to hear her truth.
"Because back then," she said, "I was waiting to be chosen." And she is not.

Craig's eyes softened. "And now?"

"Now I know I'm not waiting for anyone," she smiled. "I'm sharing space. "She was happy. Another truth discovered.

He nodded. "That's the difference. Before, we were surviving each other. Now, we're choosing each other." This was the turning point; all that they had experienced in their past, and how they saw themselves, made sense.

They didn't need to prove love anymore. It was in the way they listened, the pauses between words, the peace that wrapped itself around their shared silence. They survived their attachment and reprogrammed their way of thinking.

The Circle Completed

As they left the café, Demi stopped by the door and looked back.

"This is where it all began," she said softly.

Craig slipped his hand into hers. "And where we learned what real love looks like."

She smiled, her voice steady. "Not perfect love."

He shook his head. "No—healing love."

They stepped out into the city together, the afternoon light stretching across their path.

No tension. No chase. Just two hearts walking home—secure, connected, whole.

Reflection Section — Coming Full Circle

Coming full circle doesn't mean ending where you began—it means returning as someone transformed.

Healing doesn't erase the past; it reclaims it. You meet old versions of yourself with compassion, not shame.

For Fearful-Avoidant Healing:

You've learned that love doesn't have to be a battle between craving closeness and fearing it. Safety grows when you stay grounded even when love feels real. When you open your heart to change, you not only grow into the person you desire, but so do your connections.

For Dismissive-Avoidant Healing:

You've discovered that vulnerability doesn't threaten your independence—it deepens it. True freedom is found in connection, not in withdrawal. So connect.

Johanna's Reflection:

Every love story is also a healing story.

Craig and Demi's journey shows that when two avoidant hearts face their fears together, rather than each other, love transforms from a survival mechanism into a sanctuary.

Healing love isn't perfect—it's patient, present, and honest.

Self-Reflection Prompts:

- What does "coming full circle" mean in my own healing journey?
- How do I show love differently now that I understand my attachment patterns?
- What does "secure love" look and feel like for me today?

Epilogue
Love After the Walls

Healing doesn't end when the story does.

It continues in the quiet moments — in how you breathe through a trigger, in the way you pause before shutting down, in how you choose connection over escape.

For Craig and Demi, love became less about fixing each other and more about understanding themselves.

They learned that true healing doesn't ask you to be fearless — it asks you to stay when it feels easier to run. Changing how they viewed each other was the power that now filled their connection.

The Journey Beyond Avoidance

If you've walked this journey with them, you've witnessed what happens when two avoidant hearts meet not in chaos, but in courage.

Fearful and dismissive energies are not opposites — they are mirrors, each revealing what the other hides. And if you dare to look into the mirrors, you will find what you need to heal.

Craig's silence taught Demi patience.

Demi's emotional honesty taught Craig trust.

Together, they found balance — not in perfection, but in presence.

Healing is not a straight line; it's a circle. And those circles can take you in many directions.

Each chapter, each trigger, each step backward was part of a greater pattern — the slow weaving of safety into love. And a flourishing and loving connection.

Your Own Full Circle

Maybe you saw yourself in Demi's anxious searching, or in Craig's quiet retreat.

Perhaps you saw a little of both.

That's okay — healing is not about labeling your patterns, but learning how to hold them with compassion.

Love will still test you. Fear will still whisper. But now, you know how to listen *without losing yourself.*

You have learned the difference between intensity and intimacy, between chasing love and receiving it. You learn to love and trust yourself.

You have learned that love doesn't heal you — *you heal within love.*

From Johanna Sparrow

I wrote *Fearful Meets Dismissive* not as a story about perfection, but about persistence.

Healing avoidant love is messy, imperfect, and deeply human.

It's about rewriting the old scripts — the ones that told you you're too much, or not enough — and replacing them with truth. It's about learning to reprogram your heart and mind when life has been unkind to you and connections fail to materialize.

If this story has found its way into your hands, know that it's also an invitation:

To speak when silence feels safe.

To stay when love feels scary.

To trust that healing is possible — even for those who've built the tallest walls.

To trust without fear.

To love without needing validation.

You are no longer broken. You are becoming.

And love — the kind that heals, expands, and stays — is already finding its way toward you.

Acknowledgments

Every story about love and healing is born from truth — raw, unfiltered, and often uncomfortable truth.

This book would not exist without the people who inspired me to look deeper into what it means to love in the face of fear and avoidant patterns.

To those who've ever found themselves running from love, or waiting for someone who couldn't stay — thank you for your honesty. Your stories, shared in quiet moments or reflected in the eyes of strangers, became the heartbeat of this book for many others to learn that changing your avoidant style is possible.

To my readers — the seekers, the healers, the ones still learning to let love in — you remind me every day that healing is not a destination, it's a daily choice. A choice you must make every day.
Your courage fuels my writing, and your vulnerability gives my work purpose.

To my dear friends and creative circle — thank you for holding space for my process, for reminding me that even writers need safe spaces to land. You kept me grounded when I was too deep in the emotions of these characters, and your belief helped me push through every draft.

To those studying attachment, therapy, and human behavior, your research and compassion give us the language we need to heal the unseen wounds and bring forth healing.

And to love itself — unpredictable, stubborn, transformative love — thank you for being both the lesson and the reward.

May this book serve as a mirror, a guide, and a reminder that healing is never out of reach, even for the most avoidant of hearts.

With gratitude and grace,

Johanna Sparrow

About the Author

Johanna Sparrow has spent over two decades exploring the complex layers of human connection, attachment, relationship issues, and emotional healing that will help others. As an author, life coach, and relationship guide, she brings raw, direct honesty and compassion to every page, assisting readers to understand the hidden dynamics that shape their lives, love lives, and personal growth.

Known for her straightforward yet deeply empathetic approach, Johanna writes about what most people are afraid to admit — the fears that keep us distant, the wounds that silence our hearts, and the courage it takes to rebuild trust in their relationship. Johanna's work bridges the gap between storytelling and self-discovery, transforming emotional chaos into clarity and healing for all who seek to have a strong and flourishing relationship.

Through her books, workshops, and talks, Johanna continues to help individuals and couples recognize their patterns, embrace vulnerability, and move toward secure, lasting love.

When she's not writing, Johanna enjoys quiet mornings with her journal, engaging in deep conversations that go far beyond small talk, and the simple peace of watching the city lights fade into **the night.**

"Healing isn't about becoming someone new — it's about remembering who you were before fear taught you to hide."

— **Johanna Sparrow**

Final Notes to the Reader
From Johanna Sparrow

Healing is never a straight path. It curves, zig-zags, pauses, circles back, and sometimes stops long enough for us to catch our breath and gather strength. If you've made it this far, know that you've already done something powerful—you've faced yourself. You've walked with Craig and Demi through their moments of fear, avoidance, vulnerability, and truth. In doing so, you've also taken a look at your own with full accountability.

My hope is that Fearful Meets Dismissive gave you more than a story—it gave you a mirror. Perhaps you saw your own patterns reflected in Craig's hesitations and fear of loving, or Demi's distance. Maybe you recognized your own courage in the way they both chose to stay, even when it was painful. Healing doesn't always mean finding the perfect ending; sometimes it's learning how to stay present in the midst of imperfection because no one is perfect.

You are not broken because you've struggled to love or be loved. You are human, learning the language of safety, one brave word at a time.

Thank you for walking this journey with me. Continue to choose healing over fear and distance. Keep choosing truth. And most of all, keep choosing love that feels safe, honest, loyal, and real.

With gratitude and light,

Johanna Sparrow

www.ingramcontent.com/pod-product-compliance
Lightning Source LLC
LaVergne TN
LVHW040158080526
838202LV00042B/3216